Chuckie Meets the Beastie Bunny

by Sarah Willson
illustrated by Philip Felix, Vince Giarrano, and Byron Talman

Simon Spotlight/Nickelodeon

New York   London   Toronto   Sydney   Singapore

Based on the TV series *Rugrats*® created by Arlene Klasky, Gabor Csupo, and
Paul Germain as seen on Nickelodeon®

SIMON SPOTLIGHT
An imprint of Simon & Schuster Children's Publishing Division
1230 Avenue of the Americas
New York, New York 10020

Manufactured in the United States of America

First Edition

2 4 6 8 10 9 7 5 3 1

ISBN 0-689-83066-1

Betty DeVille finished attaching ribbons to some Easter bonnets. "Can't wait to see you kids in these bonnets!" she said to the babies. She chuckled as she stood up. "I'll go help them finish hiding the eggs for the egg hunt. Won't be long now before the Easter bunny comes!"

"Uh, Phil? Did I just hear your mom tell us that the Beastie Bunny is coming?" asked Chuckie.

"I think that's what she said," Phil replied.

"I don't like the sound of that one bit," said Chuckie. "I'm scared of bunnies! 'Specially *Beastie* Bunnies!"

"You mean, like those?" asked Phil, pointing at Tommy's grandpa's feet.

"Aaaah!" cried Chuckie.

"Or that?" asked Lil, looking at Dil's fuzzy bunny.

Dil held it up for Chuckie to see. Chuckie gulped and hid his eyes.

Just then Stu staggered upstairs from the basement. He was carrying something large and heavy on wheels.

Grandpa Lou opened his eyes. "What in tarnation is *that* contraption?" he asked.

"It's an Easter-egg decorator!" said Stu proudly. "Using special sensors, it seeks out egg-shaped objects. Then it paints them. It's programmed with seven different color choices!"

He bounded over to the coffee table and set an egg down on it. Then he hurried back to the machine and flipped a switch. It began rolling toward the coffee table.

"It's the Beastie Bunny!" Chuckie gasped.

Splat!
The machine backed away, revealing a lovely, colorful egg.
"It works!" Stu said happily.

The machine swiveled so that it pointed toward Grandpa, who had just closed his eyes again. It began to roll.

Squelp!

"Hey!" said Grandpa Lou, waking up.

"Sorry, Pop," said Stu. "Come on. I'll help you wash your head."

The machine turned and started coming toward the babies.

"The Beastie Bunny is going to color our heads just like your grandpa's, Tommy!" moaned Chuckie. "We're doomed!"

"No it won't," said Tommy. "I got a plan so we don't get decked-orated." He pulled a screwdriver out of his diaper, unlatched the playpen, and hurried over to the pile of Easter bonnets. "Put these on!" he said, tossing one to each of the babies.

The machine swiveled away from the babies and headed toward the overhead light.

"Your plan worked, Tommy!" said Phil.

"Yeah! But how long do we have to keep these bomb-its on?" demanded Lil.

"Uh-oh!" said Stu, who had come back into the room. "Pop, grab my lug wrench!"

Betty and Didi came inside just as the machine was decorating the fruit bowl.

"Stu! What on earth is going on!" Didi exclaimed.

Stu raced over to the machine and turned it off. "Oops," he said sheepishly. "I guess I still have a few kinks to work out." And with that, he wheeled it out to the backyard.

"Are you ready for the chocolate egg hunt?" Betty asked the babies, as she ushered the babies toward the back door.

"Don't forget to keep your bomb-its on," Tommy warned the others. "The Beastie Bunny won't get you, as long as you're wearing one."

"The last thing I want to do now is go looking for some eggs,"
said Chuckie firmly. "What if I find the Beastie Bunny instead?"
He sat down in the grass next to where Didi had been gardening.

"Okay, Chuckie," said Tommy. "You can stay here."

He and Phil and Lil went off to search.

Suddenly a shadow fell over Chuckie. He looked up. His Easter bonnet almost fell off. It was the Beastie Bunny!

"Oh, no!" whispered Chuckie, backing away. The Beastie Bunny rolled toward him. "I don't *want* to get decked-orated!" he said to himself. "Think, Chuckie, think!"

Suddenly Chuckie had an idea. He looked at the puddle made by the garden hose and stood up to face the machine. "Okay, Beastie Bunny!" he yelled. "Just *try* to deck-rate me!"

The Beastie Bunny rolled toward him. It toppled right into the puddle. A tiny pouf of smoke rose from it, and then the machine fell silent.

"Chuckie! You did it!" called Tommy, running over to him. "You faced the Beastie Bunny and made it stop!"

"I did, didn't I?" Chuckie grinned.

"Here," said Tommy. "Have some chocolate eggs. You earned them."

Stu came over and looked down at the machine. "Hmm. It must have shorted out. Eh. The thing didn't really work so well, anyway. I guess we'll have to color our Easter eggs the old-fashioned way. Come on, kids."

A little later Didi and Betty came into the kitchen where Stu and the babies were coloring eggs. "Goodness, Stu, what a mess!" exclaimed Didi. "I'm glad the Easter Bunny only comes once a year!"

"You see, Chuckie?" said Tommy. "My mommy just said the Beastie Bunny won't be coming back for a whole year!"

Chuckie grinned and touched the rim of his bonnet. "Well, when he does, I'll be ready!" he said.